DRUMMER BOY

MARCHING TO THE CIVIL WAR

by Ann Turner

illustrated by Mark Hess

▪ H A R P E R C O L L I N S P U B L I S H E R S

Drummer Boy

Text copyright © 1998 by Ann Turner

Illustrations copyright © 1998 by Mark Hess

Printed in the U.S.A. All rights reserved.

http://www.harperchildrens.com

Library of Congress Cataloging-in-Publication Data

Turner, Ann Warren.

   Drummer Boy / by Ann Turner ; illustrated by Mark Hess.

      p.   cm.

   Summary: A thirteen-year-old soldier, coming of age during the American Civil War, beats his drum to raise tunes and spirits and muffle the sounds of the dying.

   ISBN 0-06-027696-7. — ISBN 0-06-027697-5 (lib. bdg.)

   1. United States—History—Civil War, 1861–1865—Juvenile fiction.

[1. United States—History—Civil War, 1861–1865—Fiction.]   I. Hess, Mark, ill.

II. Title.

PZ7.T8535Dr   1998   97-14801

[E]—dc21   CIP

                                                                 AC

Typography by Al Cetta

1 2 3 4 5 6 7 8 9 10

❖

First Edition

To Marilyn Marlow,

who marches to a beat all her own

—A.T.

To my children, Elyssa, Alec, and Rachel,

in the sincere hope that one day war

will only be remembered as ancient history in books

—M.H.

The artist would like to thank Ed Vebell

for his technical advice and loan of Civil War outfits.

Who would've ever thought
I'd go to war—a boy like me?

Pa said I wasn't much use,
not like my brother Jed,
who left before me.
I was the "crow boy" in the family,
the one to throw rocks
at birds in the corn
and chase cows.

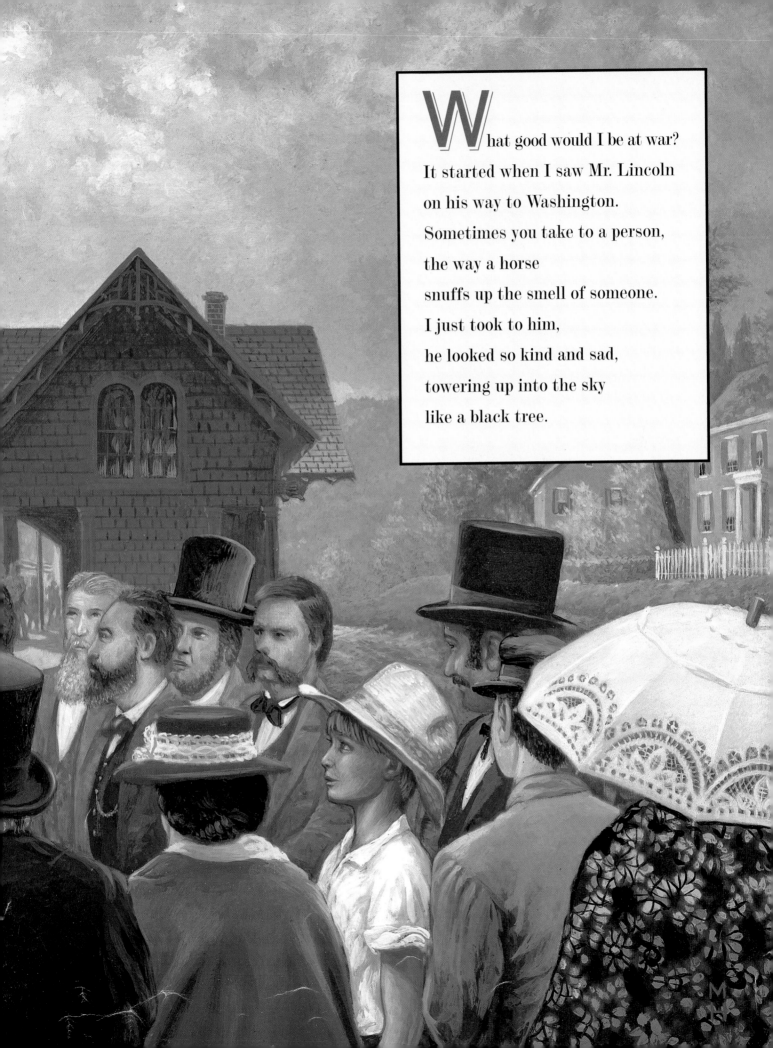

What good would I be at war?
It started when I saw Mr. Lincoln
on his way to Washington.
Sometimes you take to a person,
the way a horse
snuffs up the smell of someone.
I just took to him,
he looked so kind and sad,
towering up into the sky
like a black tree.

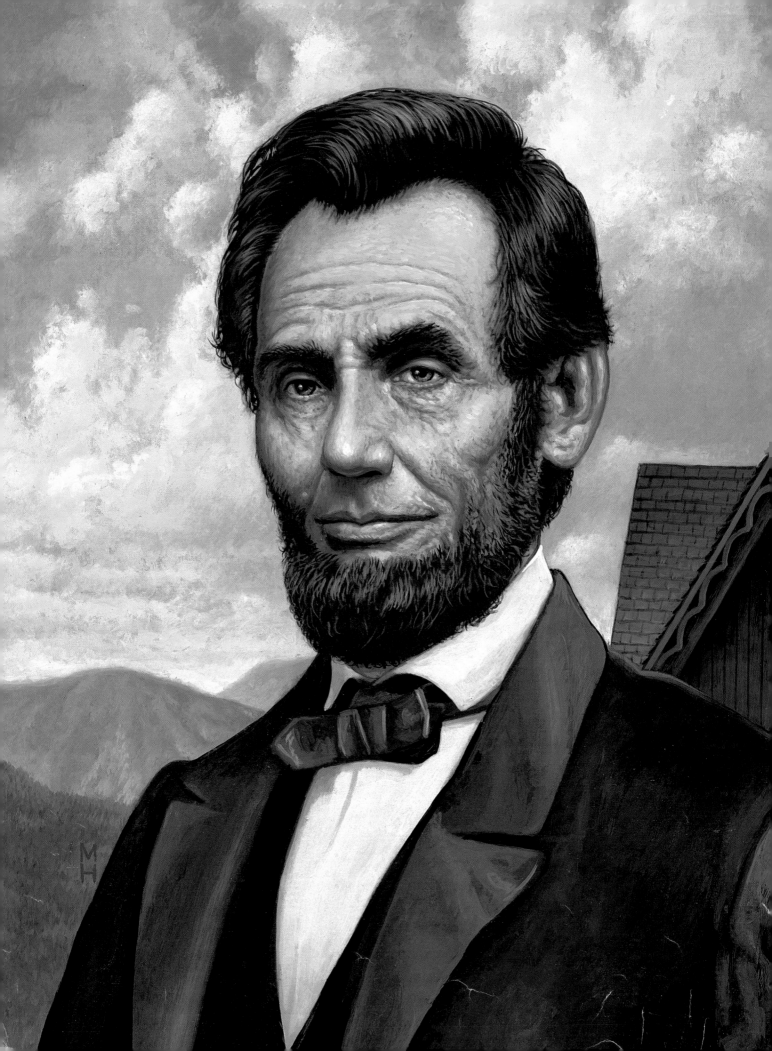

His eyes stared at me
right over the crowd,
and I thought
he was asking me to help him
keep the country together.
When I saw those ugly pictures
in the newspapers making fun of him,
I knew I had to go to war somehow,
though I wasn't old enough to fight.

Besides, I couldn't stand how
they'd got those slaves
all locked up in little houses
with nary a floor in them
or breathing space,
and sending the dogs out after the slaves
if they ever tried to get a bit of freedom.

"Our horses live better!"
I shouted at Pa,
and he told me,
"Hush! It's not your business."
But I had to go. I wrote a note to Pa,
bundled up another shirt,
a crust of bread,
and climbed out the window one night.

The next day I signed up,
told them I was fifteen—
not their business to know
I was two years short.
Man smiled at me,
said, "I like your spirit, son,
and you can be a drummer boy,
raise a tune for our men in battle."

I got shipped to training camp,
learned to slip that drum over my head
and rap a bright, marching tune
to put the spirit into our boys.

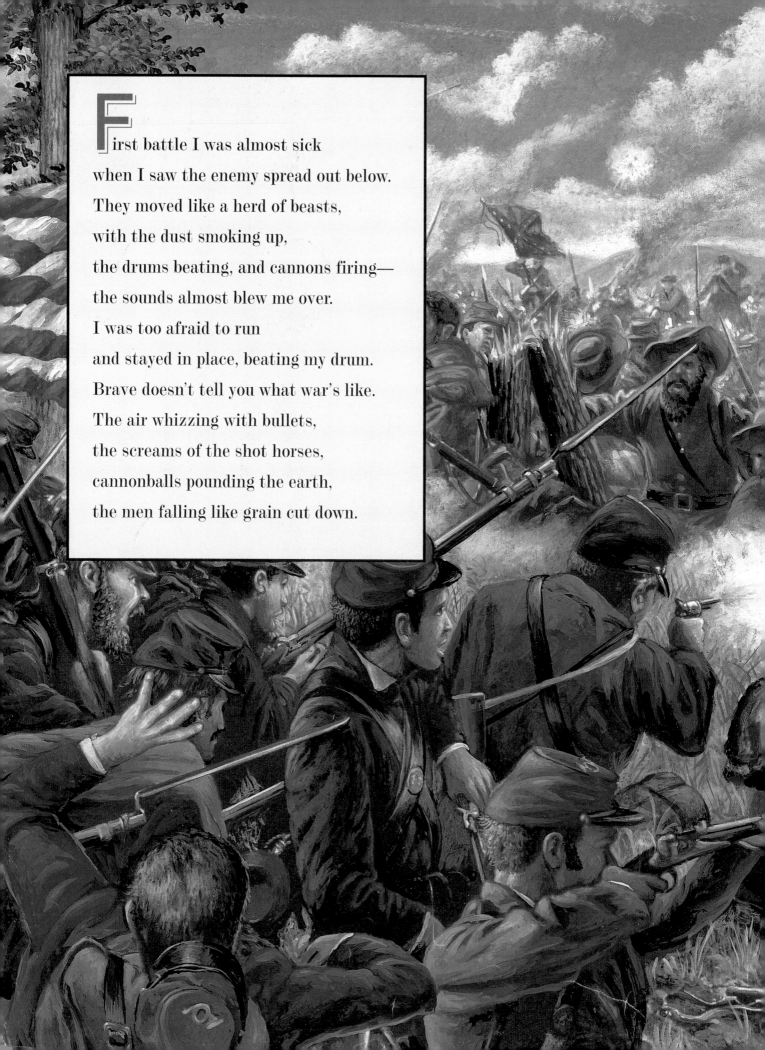

First battle I was almost sick
when I saw the enemy spread out below.
They moved like a herd of beasts,
with the dust smoking up,
the drums beating, and cannons firing—
the sounds almost blew me over.
I was too afraid to run
and stayed in place, beating my drum.
Brave doesn't tell you what war's like.
The air whizzing with bullets,
the screams of the shot horses,
cannonballs pounding the earth,
the men falling like grain cut down.

One near me cried for his mother.
I held his hand until he died,
and I always feel his fingers on mine,
how hot and dry they were,
how they grabbed mine
and crushed them
until his eyes stopped seeing.
Then I ran and hid in a hollow
until it was over,
kept my eyes shut tight
until all the sounds stopped.
That was my first battle—the worst.

Then I learned that
if I kept beating my drum
I couldn't always hear the men
crying out or the horses dying,
'cept the ground shook when they fell.
Besides, I had to stay
and relay orders to our boys.
The battles ran together in my mind
like a story too long for telling.

The worst thing is, I am beginning
to forget their faces, the boys I knew—
Sam with the hay-colored hair,
Jeff with an almost mustache,
and Abraham all the way from Maine,
who could spit tobacco
four feet to one side.
All gone now.
So at night before battle,
I go round a few campfires
to fix their faces in my mind,
the boys who might be gone by next day.

Then I do the one thing I can do.
The next morning I take my drum
and shine the brass on its side.
When it's time to go,
I march out with the drum bouncing,
rattling my sticks on the hide
so hard the sound flies up into the sky.
They tell me it makes them brave,
they tell me it covers
the first sounds of battle,
so I guess I am some use after all.

And when the war's over
and I go home,
I'll stop to talk to Mr. Lincoln
and tell him how it's his fault,
how his great, sad eyes
made me go and see things
no boy should ever see.

Being a drummer boy in the Civil War was exciting, useful, and very dangerous. It is astonishing that so many boys enlisted to be either a drummer boy or a bugler. In the Union army alone, there were about 40,000 of them, ranging in age from nine to seventeen.

A drummer boy had many duties. He woke the soldiers first thing in the morning. He might help care for horses, cook, get water, and even bury dead soldiers. But his main duty was in battle.

Each troop had its own drummer boy. When a battle started, the drummer boy beat out a long, rolling signal. Officers gave orders to their troops through different drumbeats. Even when clouds of smoke from the cannons made it impossible to see, soldiers could hear the roll of a drum telling them what to do.

Because drummer boys were so important in the Civil War, soldiers from the other side often tried to shoot them. It was a dangerous job, but many boys heard the call to go and serve their country. Some went for adventure; some went to escape the dull life on a farm; a few went to help free the slaves. Sometimes, a situation brings out resourcefulness and bravery even in the very young, and many heroes of the Civil War were, in fact, only boys.